D*ear Parent,*

*The Anne of Green Gables
teachers to raise social and
young children.*

*Anne is a strong female character with a colorful vocabulary and a
vibrant imagination. Her vocabulary level is meant to stimulate the
reading experience for young people. Inserted on the final pages
of this book is a handy dictionary for clarification of certain words
and expressions.*

*Step into Anne's world and benefit from her desire to build friendships
and inspire others through her wonderful imagination and her
determination to succeed!*

*Log on to **www.learnwithanne.com** and explore an educational
guide, with outlines of lesson plans and discussion topics available
for teachers and parents alike.*

*Also check out **www.annetoon.com** for educational games, activities
and multimedia that bring Anne's character and friends to life.*

Anne of Green Gables

Published in 2010 by Davenport Press
110 Davenport Rd.
Toronto, Ontario, M5R 3R3

Printed in Canada   ISBN = 978-0-9736803-1-7

anne OF green gables

AS SEEN ON
PBS

Anne's BABYSITTING BLUES

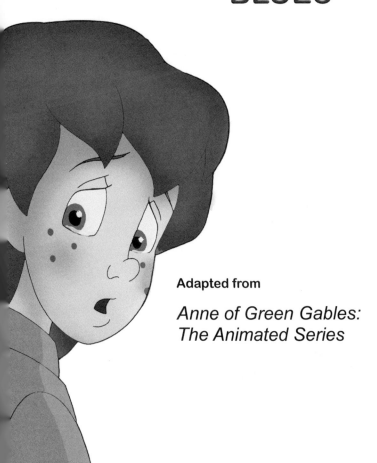

Adapted from

Anne of Green Gables:
The Animated Series

CONTENTS

Gilbert's Dilemma 6

The Grand Affair 11

Rachel's Dilemma 17

Anne's Plan 21

Getting Ready 26

Timmy Arrives 29

Toddler Troubles 33

Mrs. Van Hoit 38

A Terrible Mistake 42

The Big Mess 48

The Rattle 54

Say "Cheese" 58

Anne's Fancy Dancy Words 62

1

. . . .

Gilbert's Dilemma

It was a warm and sunny day on Prince Edward Island - the most perfect kind of day for taking pictures, or picking apples, or dreaming about fancy parties.

Gilbert looked through his camera at Anne. Anne stood with a club raised over her head. She was in her very best warrior pose. Her long red braids hung out of her Viking hat and her face was twisted into a fierce expression.

"That's perfect, Anne. Don't move!" said Gilbert. He adjusted his camera. The camera was balanced on top of a wooden board. The board lay on three broomsticks, which were tied together with an old leather belt. Gilbert had made the tripod all by himself.

"Arghhh! Hurry up!" said Anne.

"You can't rush a master," said Gilbert as he held up the flash. "I'll take it when you stop moving."

"I assure you, I am as still as a statue!" said Anne.

Gilbert looked out from under his camera. "If you're not moving, then what...oh no!"

Gilbert's tripod was tilting. He yelped and dove, and managed to catch his camera, just in time. The tripod collapsed with a bang and a clatter and a puff of dust.

"That does it!" said Gilbert. "I need a proper tripod."

"Mr. Lawson has a perfect one for sale in the general store," said Anne.

"I know, but it'll take another birthday until I have enough money to buy it. And that's a long wait."

"What you need, Gilbert, is a job," said Anne.

"That's a good idea. Except who will hire me?" he asked. Anne got back into position. But then, she and Gilbert were interrupted by some loud babbling.

"Look! Go! Appa! Appa!" A young blond toddler was walking along with Rachel Lynde, who was the best friend of Anne's adoptive mother, Marilla. He was dragging Rachel toward a display of shiny red apples. The apples were piled high, outside Mr. Lawson's store.

"Now Timmy, don't race!" warned Rachel. Her face was nearly as red as apples. She looked very tired.

"Who's Timmy?" asked Gilbert.

"Mrs. Lynde's nephew," said Anne. "He's visiting from High Water."

"She's sure got her hands full!" said Gilbert.

"I'll say. Marilla's taking Rachel to a tea party tomorrow, just to give her a break," said Anne.

"Hmm," said Gilbert. He grinned, as if he had just

thought of something really clever. And indeed, he had.

"So someone will have to look after the little tyke." Gilbert rubbed his hands together.

"Gilbert Blythe, are you thinking what I think you're thinking?" asked Anne.

"Well? Babysitting is an easy job," said Gilbert.

Suddenly, they heard a yell. They turned toward Mr. Lawson's store. Timmy had grabbed an apple at the bottom of the pyramid. All of the other apples spilled out onto the porch and down the steps.

Mr. Lawson hurried out to see what was going on, and threw up his hands when he realized what happened. Timmy grinned, delighted at the scene. He giggled. He bit into the apple in his hand. Rachel shook her head and apologized.

"I'm not sure it's so easy," said Anne.

As Rachel and Mr. Lawson discussed the damage, Timmy wandered over to Anne and Gilbert.

"Now is our chance to make an impression. Come on," said Gilbert. He waved Anne back into place, and got his camera ready.

Gilbert snapped the picture. The flash exploded with a bang, and a long trail of smoke. Timmy looked shocked for a second then he rubbed his eyes and burst into tears.

"WHAAAAA!" he screamed. "Stick go boom!"

Rachel ran over to comfort little Timmy.

"We're very sorry, Mrs. Lynde," said Anne. "We didn't think…"

"Obviously not," Rachel interrupted. "Shame on you for frightening little Timmy like that."

Rachel dried Timmy's tears and carried him off in a huff. Anne and Gilbert could do nothing but watch them go.

"Well… You certainly made an impression," said Anne.

"I lost my job before I even got it!" groaned Gilbert.

2

. . . .

The Grand Affair

Later that afternoon, Anne sat on the porch of Green Gables. She was holding a party invitation that was embossed with a fancy gold pattern.

"Mrs. Van Hoit cordially invites you and a guest to a tea party at her home on Friday afternoon," Anne read. She pressed the card to her chest in awe and sighed.

"I'd simply bust if I were ever invited to such a grand affair."

Marilla grabbed the invitation from Anne on her way past.

"Bust, would you? Then it's a good thing I'm taking Rachel Lynde." Marilla tucked the invitation into her apron.

"But didn't she get her own invitation?" Anne asked.

"She declined, thinking she would be too preoccupied with little Timmy," Marilla answered, picking up the broom to sweep the porch.

"Mrs. Van Hoit's house is the grandest in Avonlea," she said. She waved her hands in the air. "I'd give anything to have a peak inside."

"Four walls and a roof," shrugged Marilla. "It's the same as any other house."

"Oh Marilla. I know you're only saying that to lighten

the crushing disappointment I feel at not being able to accompany you."

Marilla chuckled softly as she swept the dirt off the porch.

"If your greatest ambition is to set eyes on Mrs. Van Hoit's parlour, I have no doubt that you'll one day achieve it." Marilla rested the broom on the side of the porch. She wiped her hands on her apron, and turned to go into the house.

Suddenly, Anne's best friend, Diana, came racing up the path toward Green Gables. She was waving a piece of paper in the air. "My mother got an invitation to the Van Hoits!" she yelled.

"Marilla got one, too," said Anne.

"And?" said Diana, climbing the front steps. Anne sat down and rested her chin in her hand. "And she's taking Rachel Lynde." Diana sat down next to Anne.

"My mother's taking my Aunt Josephine." Anne jumped up, refusing to despair.

"Then we'll have to imagine what it's like to be invited to the most opulent house in Avonlea."

Diana giggled. Anne plucked the invitation out of Diana's hand and pretended she had never seen it before.

"Oh my! An invitation to the Van Hoits? 'And guest?' Why, whomever shall I bring?" Anne asked, in her best, old rich lady voice. She sighed, and pretended to struggle for the answer.

Diana sat up straighter and raised her eyebrows.

"I wonder..." she said.

Anne looked out into the distance, and smiled.

"I know, my dear friend... Matthew!"

Diana turned around, and saw Matthew, Marilla's brother, pass them on his way to the barn.

"I don't go in much for fancy do's," he said.

"Hmm," said Anne. "Then I'll just have to invite..." Anne scratched her chin. She squinted her eyes.

"Ahem," said Diana. She stood up, smiled, and straightened her dress.

"Gilbert!" said Anne.

Diana's smile slid off of her face. She threw up her arms and sat back down in a huff. Meanwhile, Gilbert walked up to the porch.

"Did you get the babysitting job?" Anne asked him.

"Face it," said Gilbert. "I don't have a chance."

"Wish I could help, but I can't even get invited to a pretend party," sniffed Diana.

Gilbert sat down next to Diana. "I've never babysat before. Why should she give me this break?" he shrugged.

"Don't you think you should get the job before you take a break," joked Diana.

Anne jumped up and got Gilbert to his feet.

"Of course you're worthy of the job. You're old enough. You're a boy of... well, moderate intelligence."

"Whoa!" Gilbert protested.

"And Mrs. Lynde has known you since you were Timmy's age. In fact, now that I think of it, you're utterly perfect for the job," said Anne.

"You're right! I am," said Gilbert. He beamed.

"You march over there right now and tell her she'd be a fool not to hire you!" said Anne. She walked Gilbert to the gate.

"Gee, thanks," said Gilbert, as he walked off.

"Do you really think he can handle it?" Diana asked Anne as soon as Gilbert was out of earshot.

"Not a chance," Anne quickly replied. The girls giggled.

3

Rachel's Dilemma

Gilbert walked to Rachel's house. He took a deep breath and knocked on her door. Rachel swung the door open. Timmy was running around her feet, dragging his blue blanket behind him.

"Gilbert, what brings you here?" she asked.

"Well, Mrs. Lynde..."

"Have you come to flash us with your new-fangled apparatus?" she asked.

"No, ma'am!" said Gilbert. He looked down and watched as Timmy wrapped the blanket around himself.

"I'm afraid I'm in a tizzy right now," Rachel continued. "Mrs. Petty rudely went and caught a cold, leaving me without a babysitter tomorrow. If I don't find a replacement, I'll miss the social event of the year!"

Rachel went to take a step backward, but her feet got caught up in the blanket, and she began to fall! Gilbert leapt forward and caught her just in time.

"Ah. Well. Thank you, Gilbert," Rachel said, straightening herself up. She looked at her watch. "I best be going now."

But Gilbert couldn't let her leave yet!

"I know just the person for the job, Mrs. Lynde," Gilbert blurted out. "Someone reliable. Someone old enough. Someone you've known for a long time."

"Who?" she asked, "Sounds perfect. When can I meet this person?"

"Ta-da!" said Gilbert. "You already have!"

Rachel looked puzzled for a few seconds. Then she began to laugh.

"You? Gilbert, what experience do you have babysitting?" she asked.

"Well, I've... I've played with my cousins a hundred times," said Gilbert.

"There's a big difference between playing games and being entirely responsible for my precious nephew!" said Rachel.

Gilbert had never thought about it that way. Maybe he wasn't perfect for the job.

"Oh," Gilbert said sadly. "Maybe you're right."

"Of course I'm right," Rachel agreed. "I'm always right."

Rachel quickly started to close the door. "Thank

you for your interest Gilbert. Should any more suitable babysitters come to mind, please don't hesitate to send them my way." With that, Rachel slammed the door in Gilbert's face.

4

Anne's Plan

Gilbert slumped back to Green Gables and told Anne and Diana what had happened. "Utterly unacceptable," Anne complained.

Diana put away the party invitation carefully. She shrugged, "Well, if he's had no experience, it makes sense."

Gilbert looked up and scowled, "How am I supposed to get experience if nobody will take a chance on me?"

"When I had to look after those wretched souls at the orphanage nobody thought to inquire about my experience!" said Anne.

Gilbert tried putting his tripod back together. He set it upright and then took a step back.

"There. Maybe I don't need a job after all!" But suddenly, the tripod creaked and started to lean to one side. The whole thing toppled over, sending a great big poof of dust into the air.

Anne bent to pick up the pieces. "If you ask me, Rachel Lynde is being entirely unreasonable. I'm going to march over there right now and tell her as much!"

"Bravo Anne!" Diana cheered.

"Uh, Anne...are you sure?" Gilbert asked nervously.

"Trust me Gil. I know just how to handle Mrs Lynde," Anne told him confidently.

Anne marched all the way to Rachel's house. She walked right up her front steps and knocked on the door.

Rachel opened the door. Timmy stood at her side, clutching at her skirt.

"Yes?"

"Mrs. Lynde," Anne said, "I am here to speak to you regarding the question of your need for a babysitter. I ask you to remember," she continued, "that I say this having looked after dozens of children at the orphanage. In my opinion, you've been offered the perfect person for the job."

"I certainly have!" smiled Rachel. "Thank you, Anne. I'll expect you tomorrow afternoon."

"Me? No, but Mrs. Lynde..." But Rachel had already slammed the door. "I meant Gilbert!" Anne shouted.

Suddenly, Gilbert appeared at the bottom of Rachel's porch steps.

"So? What did she say?" he asked. Anne couldn't let Gilbert down, so she turned and knocked once more on Rachel's door.

"Anne? Gilbert? Please, I'm very busy," Rachel said. "What can I do for you?"

"Please, Mrs. Lynde," Anne pleaded. " Can we speak to you about exactly who it is who will be watching Timmy?"

"Oh, all right," said Rachel. "Both of you come inside."

Rachel led them into the living room where they both took a seat on the couch. Gilbert pulled Timmy onto his lap and began bouncing him on his knee. Meanwhile, Anne tried to explain the situation.

"Mrs. Lynde, I assure you, it's Gilbert you want, not me."

"How do you mean?" asked Rachel. She leaned forward in her chair.

"Gilbert could babysit Timmy at Green Gables," said Anne.

"Then, Anne could help out," added Gilbert.

"And Matthew would be nearby in the fields the whole time if we need help from a grown-up," said Anne.

"Well," Rachel said, sinking back into her chair. "Now that you put it that way, I suppose..."

"Hooray!" cheered Gilbert, momentarily letting go of Timmy, who slid off Gilbert's knee to the ground. Timmy started to whine.

Rachel crossed her arms and glared at Gilbert, and then at Anne. They chuckled sheepishly.

Luckily Timmy decided that sliding off Gilbert's knee was a fun game. "More, more!" he shouted.

Rachel walked Anne and Gilbert to the door. "I'll drop Timmy off at Green Gables tomorrow at noon. Don't be late," she warned.

Rachel closed the door and Gilbert jumped for joy. "Wahoo! My first job. It was hard work, but it was worth it!" he said.

"Getting a job is just the beginning," said Anne. "Now, the real work starts!"

5

. . . .

Getting Ready

Gilbert and Anne went back to Green Gables. It was time to Timmy-proof the house. Anne carried Marilla's fancy punch bowl into the dining room. The table was stacked high with all sorts of household breakables.

"I appreciate you helping me with my first job, Ms. Cuthbert," said Gilbert.

Marilla took the bowl from Anne and placed it on the table. "It would have been nice had certain people conferred with me before making so magnanimous an offer!" She shot Anne a look.

"Believe me, Marilla. I had to think fast. We didn't have the time," Anne explained.

"Green Gables is hardly set up for a toddler to run rampant in," Marilla said. "We got you at a relatively civilized age."

Matthew entered the room. He was carrying a porcelain vase. "So we just take anything that might break or hurt the little boy, and put it out of harm's way…"

Gilbert picked up a bowl of pennies from the table. "But these pennies won't break," he said.

"Maybe not, but toddlers can choke on small objects," explained Matthew.

"Speaking of toddler's tummies…," said Marilla as she walked towards the kitchen, "All cleaners and such must be safely locked away."

Anne walked over to the kitchen stove. "Pot handles get turned in," she said.

Matthew put all of the knives in a high drawer. "And sharp things kept out of reach," he said.

Gilbert nodded, eyes wide. "Golly," he said. "There are so many dangers for little children, it's a wonder any of them survive!"

"I'm sorry Marilla. I didn't realize how much work this would be for you," Anne apologized.

"We'll manage," said Marilla. She pulled an old wooden rattle from her apron pocket. "I found something that might amuse the child!"

Matthew stared at the rattle, surprised. "My old baby rattle! I haven't seen that in a donkey's age!"

Marilla rolled her eyes. She handed the rattle to Anne. "It must have been a rather old donkey," she said.

Anne shook the rattle. "Oh, Marilla. You can be sure we'll treat this treasured family heirloom with the utmost of care!" Anne put the rattle in her apron.

6

. . . .

Timmy Arrives

Anne watched as Marilla finished pinning up her hair for Mrs. Van Hoit's tea party.

"How lovely you look, Marilla," Anne sighed. "I shall have to be content imagining what I would have worn if I had such a special event to attend."

Marilla slid the last hairpin into place. "Anne, one day there will be many tea parties for you to go to. In the meantime you've made a commitment to mind Timmy with Gilbert."

"I know." Anne replied. "Oh Marilla! You should wear your brooch for this occasion!" Anne reached into Marilla's jewelry box and handed her the brooch just as the sound of the front door opening and Timmy's little feet running into the front hall could be heard.

Marilla fixed the brooch to her shawl and followed Anne down the stairs to greet their guests.

Rachel drove her horse and buggy to Green Gables to drop off little Timmy.

"Here's Timmy's blanket... and toys... and favorite snacks..." Rachel handed each of the items to Anne, who was straining to carry everything. She peered out over the top of the pile, but soon her view was blocked.

"His diapers and a stuffed animal - named Alphonse or Albert, I can't remember - and a change of clothes... Now what am I forgetting?"

Marilla climbed into the buggy. "Nothing, I'm sure," she said. "Come on, we have a tea party to get to."

Anne stumbled as she struggled to peek out from behind Timmy's things.

"Marilla," she gasped. "Promise to remember every detail! I want a full report, down to the last cucumber sandwich and lace trim!"

"I will Anne. You two have fun."

"I'm rather excited myself," Rachel confided in Marilla. "Now that I know little Timmy is in good hands."

Marilla and Rachel went off. They waved as the carriage passed by Matthew, who was walking toward the barn. "I'm in the field if you need me," he called.

Anne and Gilbert were left standing in the dust.

Gilbert put Timmy down at his feet.

"What a big fuss everybody's making. After all, there are two of us and only one of…" Gilbert's voice trailed off when he realized that Timmy was nowhere to be seen. "Where did he go?"

"They're not called toddlers for nothing!" said Anne. And Gilbert scrambled to catch little Timmy.

"Come back here, you rascal!" said Gilbert. Timmy was headed towards the large brown and white cow.

"Oh no!" Gilbert gasped. "Not Grumpy Gussy!"

Timmy giggled, and got right underneath Grumpy Gussy.

"No Timmy!" yelled Gilbert.

Timmy turned, suddenly, to see who was calling his name. He lost his balance and flailed about. He grabbed onto Gussy's udder to catch his balance.

Gussy let out a long and loud 'moo'. She was clearly very upset. Gilbert managed to grab Timmy.

He pulled him out of the way, just as Gussy was getting ready to kick.

"I've got a feeling this is going to be a long afternoon!" said Gilbert.

1

....

Toddler Troubles

Timmy sat at the kitchen table. He was covered in mud.

"What a mess!" said Anne.

"All Timmy needs is a bath," said Gilbert.

Anne shot him a look. "Have you ever given a toddler a bath?" she asked.

"How hard can it be?"

Anne prepared the bath water. When the kettle whistled, she poured the hot water into the bath basin. She added some cold water. Then she felt the water with her pinky finger. "Not too hot and not too cold," she said.

Gilbert lowered Timmy into the water. "No baff, no baff!" he cried, and squirmed to get out of Gilbert's arms.

"Sorry chum," said Gilbert, struggling to shove the toddler into the tub. "You have to take a bath, you are covered in mud."

"Here, Timmy," said Anne. "Look what I found! It's your little sail boat! I bet your sail boat would love to have a bath with you!"

Gilbert lowered Timmy into the water. Timmy kicked and squealed. He splashed Gilbert. He splashed Anne. In fact, he managed to splash the entire kitchen.

When it was time for Timmy to finish his bath, Anne had difficulty getting him out of the tub. He was having too much fun!

"But Timmy," Gilbert said. "I have all these toys here, and no one to play with!" Timmy's eyes grew wide as he quickly changed his mind. Gilbert pulled him out of the tub and dried him off.

"Nice trick, Gil," Anne congratulated him.

"I learned from the best," he answered, winking at her. "Now Timmy, I bet you don't know how to put on your shirt all by yourself!" Timmy hurried to prove Gilbert wrong. Anne was very impressed.

A little while later, a very clean Timmy beat on a pot with a wooden spoon, while Anne made some porridge.

"Well, at least Timmy's clean!" Anne shouted over Timmy's "music".

Suddenly the banging stopped. Anne smiled. "Finally, I thought he'd never stop."

Gilbert's eyes rested on the pot and spoon. "I wish he hadn't," he said. Timmy was nowhere to be found. Anne and Gilbert raced out of the kitchen.

They finally found Timmy. He was sitting underneath the dining room table. This was the same dining room table where they had placed all of the breakables.

Timmy was tugging on the white linen tablecloth. Every time Timmy pulled on the cloth, the breakables came an inch closer to smashing to the floor.

"Timmy, no!" yelled Anne.

Gilbert grabbed Timmy. Anne dove to catch the punch bowl. She was just in time. And the entire dish of pennies toppled. It rained all over Anne.

"Great catch!" Gilbert congratulated her, laughing.

"From now on, this door stays closed," grumbled Anne. She shook some of the pennies from her apron. They all left the dining room. Anne slammed the door shut, and locked it.

Gilbert took Timmy out to the porch. They played
with some blocks together. Soon after, Anne joined
them. She brought two steaming mugs of hot cocoa.

"Here's some hot cocoa to fortify you," said Anne.

Timmy tried to grab for it, but Gilbert raised it out
of his reach. He put the mug to his lips. He took a sip.

"Delicious," said Gilbert.

Anne shrugged. "I only wish it were tea in a fancy

cup at Mrs. Van Hoit's house," she sighed.

"What's the big deal, anyway?" asked Gilbert.

"That's just it," she replied with a sigh. "I don't know."

"I'm sorry you're stuck here with me, Anne, but I really appreciate you helping me babysit," Gilbert said.

Anne felt bad. She didn't mean to make Gilbert feel guilty.

"Oh, Gil. I don't mind helping you babysit at all! I wasn't even invited to the tea party. You and Timmy are wonderful company - Timmy!" Anne cried. Suddenly Timmy was racing off across the lawn.

"The fun just never ends with a toddler, does it?" huffed Gilbert jokingly as he raced to catch up with Timmy.

"If you think he's difficult," Anne shouted, catching up, "You should try watching twins!"

8

. . . .

Mrs. Van Hoit

Anne stared off into the distance, and tried to imagine what was going on at Mrs. Van Hoit's house. If only she were able to be there! Mrs.Van Hoit would be wearing her finest dress.

"More tea, my pet?" Mrs. Van Hoit would ask.

"Just a spot more, Mrs. Van Hoit," Anne would answer. "And when you have a moment, may I have a tour of your house?" Anne would ask.

"But of course. I would be happy to show you around," Mrs. Van Hoit would say and the two would be off. And what a tour it would be!

"When I heard you were indisposed for my tea party I thought the thing to do was to have you over on your own, so it would be just the two of us," Mrs. Van Hoit said.

There would be china vases, large and small, and

fancy carpets, and glamorous people holding fans. Anne would see a bell pull hanging off to the side. "What does this do?" she would ask.

"Only one way to find out," Mrs. Van Hoit would say. Anne would smile, and then yank the bell pull. A shower of rose petals would fall down. Anne would put out her arms and twirl.

"Rose petals!" she cried in glee. "The rich really are different!"

A voice interrupted Anne's daydream.

"Anne, hey, Anne?" called Diana.

Anne opened her eyes, and blinked a few times. She looked around. Of course, she was still on the porch of the house at Green Gables.

"Hi, Diana!" she said.

"How is babysitting?" asked Diana.

"Gilbert's done wonders," said Anne. "You'd never guess he had no experience."

"You mean he would be able to manage on his own?" asked Diana.

"Oh, yes," said Anne. "I'm sure of it."

Diana leapt up onto the porch, delighted. "That means that you can come to a party!" she said. Diana pulled a piece of paper from her apron. It was white with gold writing. It was an invitation to Mrs. Van Hoit's!

"Where did this come from?" gasped Anne.

Diana smiled. "Mother caught that cold from Mrs. Petty, so she can't go. Which means, now is our chance!"

"I would love to go to the party with you, Diana, but

I have to stay here," said Anne.

"But you said yourself that Gilbert is doing a fine job," said Diana.

"Matthew's just out in the field," said Diana. "He'll be able to help Gilbert, should anything go wrong."

Anne looked out into the field. Matthew was definitely within shouting distance.

"It's okay Anne," Gilbert said. "Everything is under control now."

Diana held the beautiful invitation. Gilbert held Timmy. Anne looked from Diana to Gilbert. What could possibly go wrong?

"Oh! Let me get my good shoes!" she said. She turned and ran into the house.

9

. . . .

A Terrible Mistake

Anne and Diana skipped to Mrs. Van Hoit's house. Anne paused when she reached the path to the front door. She looked up.

"There it is Diana - the finest house on this side of Charlottetown!" said Anne.

The girls were so excited; they ran up to the front door. They paused to straighten out their clothes. Then Anne pulled the tasseled cord hanging outside. Bells jingled and clanged.

"I hope I'm not too dazzled," Anne told Diana. "Marilla says luxury can stupefy even the most calm of us."

"We best keep a cool head," agreed Diana.

"If not, we can douse it in Mrs. Van Hoit's waterfall!"

The girls giggled. Suddenly the front door swung

open. A butler looked down at them. They curtseyed nervously. "Er… Miss Shirley and Miss Barry," said Diana.

....

Back at Green Gables, Timmy was bawling. Gilbert held him and paced.

"What's the matter? Think, Gilbert. What makes a toddler cry? Oh no!" he said. He glanced at Timmy's diaper. Luckily, it was still clean.

"Okay, maybe you're hungry," said Gilbert.

"Hung-ee!" Timmy yelled.

"Well, why didn't you say so?" said Gilbert.

Gilbert brought Timmy to the kitchen. He placed him in a highchair. Gilbert placed a bowl of beans in front of Timmy.

"I hope you like beans!" said Gilbert.

Matthew peeked into the kitchen. "How's it going in here?" he asked.

"Everything is under control," said Gilbert.

"Good job. You know where I am if you need me," said Matthew.

Gilbert was so proud. He leaned into Timmy. "Did

you hear that? Good job. What do you think about that?"
Timmy picked up a spoonful of beans. He stared at
the beans. He stared at Gilbert. And then he let out a
squeal. He flung the beans at Gilbert's face.

"Ugh!" said Gilbert. "Beans!" He wiped his face.

....

Anne and Diana entered Mrs. Van Hoit's house,
shaking with excitement. "Wait!" cried Anne, just before
stepping into the foyer. "I'm going to close my eyes so
that I can drink in all the exquisite beauty of the rich
when I look around for the first time."

Diana led Anne through the threshold into the sitting
room.

"Stand me where I'll get the full effect," she said to
Diana. "Oh, I have imagined this moment in-depth! I
wonder if it will be exactly as I had envisioned it?"

Diana looked around. Her eyes were wide. "Anne, I
hate to tell you," she began.

"Is this the perfect vantage point?" asked Anne.
"I want to be surrounded in splendor when I open my
eyes."

"Uh...as good a place as any," Diana answered
hesitantly.

But Anne wasn't listening. "And now," she said, "The moment of truth. After this, I might never be content with Green Gables again!"

Anne took a deep breath and opened her eyes. Anne and Diana were in the middle of an ordinary sitting room. There were lots of ladies milling about, drinking tea. But other than that, it was just like any other room, in any other house, in all of Charlottetown. She gasped with surprise.

"Why, there's nothing spectacular about this at all!" gasped Anne.

"In fact," added Diana, "It's rather dull."

And indeed, Mrs. Van Hoit's sitting room was no more spectacular than any other house in Avonlea, just as Marilla had said. The walls were wall-papered in a pretty flower paper and adorned with framed family photographs. A reasonably stylish rug covered the floor and a couple of slightly worn couches furnished the room. This was not at all what Anne had envisioned. Only one article in the room saved Anne from her extreme disappointment.

"Oh Diana!" she gasped. "Look at the table! First things first. A cream cake before introductions."

They walked to the table piled high with food.

Cucumber sandwiches, juicy strawberries, scones

and chocolate tarts… there were no end to the goodies in sight! Each girl helped themselves to some goodies.

Just then, Diana pointed toward the staircase. Rachel was there. She was talking so loudly that her voice drifted all the way to where the girls were eating. Anne perked her ears up when she heard her name.

"I'll have you know, if it weren't for Marilla's Anne over at Green Gables, I wouldn't be here at all," said Rachel.

"I hear she's quite the responsible young lady," said Mrs. Van Hoit.

"Yes," said Marilla. "Thankfully, my influence has tempered her wild spirit."

Anne grimaced. Diana put her hand over her mouth to hide her giggle.

Rachel continued. "One thing's for sure - I'd never have allowed Gilbert to babysit my precious nephew if I thought for a second that Anne wasn't by his side."

"Too true," said Mrs. Van Hoit. "Excellent judgement. More tea, ladies?"

Anne gulped. "Oh, Diana! I've made a terrible mistake!"

10

. . . .

A Big Mess

Gilbert fed the last spoonful of beans to Timmy. He glanced around the room. The kitchen was a mess. Timmy was a mess. And Gilbert was a mess, too.

"There! You've eaten it all!" congratulated Gilbert.

Timmy began to squirm and fidget.

"Now what? What's wrong?" asked Gilbert. Timmy stopped squirming. He let out a huge belch. Gilbert sighed.

. . . .

Anne and Diana tried to scramble out of Mrs. Van Hoit's house without getting caught. They crawled through the sitting room on their hands and knees.

"We have to get back to Green Gables," whispered Anne. "I should never have left Gilbert to manage on his own," said Anne.

"But Gilbert was doing so well," said Diana.

"Things can change in a blink of an eye. What if something went wrong?" Anne asked.

Anne and Diana turned a corner. The path was clear, so they made a dash for the door. But then, a pair of shiny shoes stepped into their way. They stopped short.

They looked up, slowly. The butler was looming over them. Anne smiled sweetly at him. "Just looking for the door," she said.

The butler gave them a disapproving look, but sidestepped out of their way. He waited until after they scampered out the door to chuckle softly at their antics.

....

Gilbert walked across the front yard of Green Gables. Timmy waddled beside him.

"Timmy," started Gilbert. "Babysitting is a lot like life. It's full of ups and downs. My first job taught me that every problem has a solution." Gilbert looked down to smile at Timmy. But Timmy was no longer next to him.

"Boy, are you unpredictable!"

Gilbert looked around frantically. He saw Timmy crawling up the ramp into the hen house. Timmy managed to squeeze in. The hens squawked and squawked. Gilbert raced over.

"Come on out, Timmy!" Gilbert called. He stuck his head through the hen hole. An angry hen flew from her nest. An egg rolled out of the nest and dropped towards the floor, but Gilbert managed to catch it in the nick of time. Timmy smiled at Gilbert. Gilbert couldn't help but smile back.

....

Anne and Diana managed to escape from Mrs. Van Hoit's house. They ran back to Green Gables.

"I'm sure Timmy will be fine," said Diana.

"If not, I'll never forgive myself," said Anne.

They raced through the gate. "Gilbert? Gilbert? Where are you?" called Anne.

Gilbert stumbled out of the hen house. He was covered in feathers. "Anne, hi! You're back so soon…"

"Where's little Timmy?" asked Anne.

"Well," shrugged Gilbert. "Um. He's inside there." Gilbert pointed to the hen house.

"Inside there!" squealed Diana. "Oh Gilbert! Toddlers should not play in chicken coops."

"I didn't put him in there," Gilbert defended himself. "He climbed in on his own."

Anne pushed past Gilbert and marched to the hen house. "I should have known better than to let you alone with Timmy."

She peered inside. Timmy was sleeping soundly in a hen's nest. A hen clucked quietly nearby.

"Shhh, you'll wake him. It was the only place I could get him to take a nap," explained Gilbert.

Anne was impressed. "With that kind of creativity, you'll be the best babysitter, ever!"

Gilbert lifted Timmy gently from the nest. Then they all walked into the kitchen. Anne looked around in amazement.

"The best babysitter," she said. "But a terrible housekeeper!"

Anne grabbed a mop, a rag and a dustpan. She filled a bucket with soapy water and handed it to Gilbert.

"Here Gilbert," she instructed. "You can start mopping the hall and the kitchen floor."

Anne turned towards Diana. "You can work on the walls," she told her.

Anne peered down at Timmy, who was watching quietly at her feet. "Timmy," Anne addressed the toddler. "Want to play a fun game?"

Timmy squealed his approval and climbed to his feet. "Let's see how quickly you can collect all your toys and put them in the basket!"

Timmy began scurrying around the kitchen, collecting each toy one by one and putting them in the wicker basket that Rachel had brought over.

"Wow, Anne," said Gilbert. "That's a great trick."

"Sadly, I have years of babysitting up my sleeve," replied Anne. "That will keep him busy for a little while, and hopefully tire him out. I'll scrub down the walls and everywhere else he splashed his beans."

"Then we better work together on the dishes," concluded Gilbert.

Anne, Gilbert and Timmy worked as a team to get Green Gables back to ship shape condition. When they were done, all three of them were ready for a nap!

II

. . . .

The Rattle

Rachel and Marilla returned to Green Gables.

"Timmy looks none the worse for his visit to Green Gables. Hello Timmy!" she said.

"Thank you, Mrs. Lynde," said Gilbert.

Marilla looked at Anne. "You haven't asked one question about Mrs. Van Hoit's tea party," she said.

"Anne has been so busy helping me, she must have forgotten all about the party," Gilbert said.

"Well, her house was, as I expected, no better than last year," said Marilla.

"And her cream cakes aren't nearly as good as yours... or so I'm told," said Anne.

Marilla looked at Anne. She had a puzzled expression on her face. "Timmy should have a memento of his visit. May I have Matthew's old baby rattle?" asked Marilla.

"What a wonderful idea," said Anne. "Now where is it?" she patted her apron. The pockets were empty. Where had the rattle gone?

"Oh dear. It must have fallen out when... when..." Anne struggled to come up with an answer. She looked around at the others. She slumped her shoulders and sighed.

"When, what?" asked Marilla.

"When Diana and I were crawling to escape Mrs. Van Hoit's," Anne admitted.

"You neglected your responsibilities?" gasped Rachel.

"We were escaping to come back here!" said Diana.

"Except Anne never should have left in the first place," said Marilla. "It's a good thing Gilbert is so responsible!"

"Marilla. It was a dreadful mistake. I assure you, I'll never make it again. It's just that Diana's mother could not go to Mrs. Van Hoit's party, and it was the perfect opportunity to fulfill my dream of attending a real grown-up tea party!" Anne tried to explain. "And Gilbert was doing such a fantastic job with Timmy, that I knew he could handle it on his own!"

"I'll say!" said Rachel as Timmy scrambled across the floor and threw himself into Gilbert's arms.

"Gil! Gil!" squealed Timmy.

"Well, Anne," said Rachel. "No harm came to my precious nephew, and it does seem that you've learnt your lesson."

"Oh yes, Mrs. Lynde," agreed Anne. "I certainly will never neglect my responsibilities again!"

"And we'll begin that promise with some extra chores tomorrow," Marilla concluded, patting Anne's shoulder. "Just to help that lesson sink in."

"It would be my honour," said Anne, "but it's a shame that Matthews rattle was needlessly sacrificed for me to learn my lesson."

Marilla smiled. She pulled the rattle out of her own pocket.

"Not necessarily!" she said.

"Marilla, you knew!" said Anne. She gave Marilla a hug.

"Anne Shirley, you do beat all," Marilla said.

12

. . . .

Say Cheese

The very next morning, Gilbert knocked on the front door of Green Gables.

Anne answered, wearing her cleaning apron and carrying a broom.

"I'm just finishing the last of my morning chores," she told him. "I just need to sweep the porch and then we can go."

Gilbert took the broom from her. "I'll sweep the porch for you," he said. "It's the least I can do after you helping me get the job."

Anne smiled thankfully, but took the broom back again.

"I appreciate that Gilbert, but I have already learned my lesson about neglecting my responsibilities. Besides, it was my pleasure helping out a friend."

Anne quickly swept the porch and soon the two were off, walking down the road towards Mr. Lawson's store to buy Gilbert's new tripod.

"The babysitting money and my savings were just enough!" he said. He attached his camera to the tripod. "I can't wait to try it out!"

"Whose picture will you take first?" asked Anne.

Rachel turned the corner. She had Timmy in tow.

Gilbert ran over to greet them. He tousled Timmy's hair. Timmy smiled back up at Gilbert and took his hand.

"Hey, chum. Are you ready?" Gilbert asked him.

"You'll have plenty of extra money for your hobby now, Gilbert," said Rachel. "I've spread the word and I expect with my glowing recommendation people will be lining up for your services!"

Even as Rachel said this, a mother with a young child waited by Mr. Lawson's store, hoping to ask for Gilbert's help as a babysitter.

Gilbert picked up Timmy and smiled.

"It's thanks to you giving me a chance, Mrs. Lynde. You gave me the experience I needed to learn how to be a good babysitter. And Anne was a great teacher," he added.

Well, I always knew you had it in you, Gilbert," Mrs. Lynde said. "You should be confident in your own abilities."

"Hey, Gilbert, say cheese!" called Anne.

Timmy and Gilbert smiled for the camera. This time when the flash exploded, Timmy didn't cry at all.

Anne's Fancy Dancy Words

Adorned – decorated with
Ambition – to have a goal
Antics – silly or playful tricks
Apparatus – a group of tools or objects that work together to do a job
Babbling – the noises a baby makes when trying to speak
Conferred – consulted, shared information or opinions
Douse – to put out a flame with water or to turn off a light
Embossed – decorated
Envisioned – imagined
Fidget – moving around to avoid sitting still
Flailed – to swing your arms when losing balance
Fortify – to make something strong
Foyer – the first room or entrance of a house
Frantically – worriedly, desperately
Grimaced – a facial expression showing pain
Heirloom – old treasure passed down through generations
Indisposed – unwell or unavailable
Inquire – to ask a question
Opulent – wealthy, rich
Magnanimous – generous, noble
Milling – to move around slowly

Neglected – did not look after, forgot
Nick of time – means "just in time"
New fangled – a new fashion or idea
Preoccupied – busy
Puzzled – confused
Rampant – wild, without boundaries
Scurrying – to move or race quickly
Sheepishly – to be embarrassed
Splendor – beauty
Stupefy – to stun, shock or overwhelm
Tasseled – when a cord or curtain is decorated with
a bunch of hanging threads at the bottom
Tempered – softened, calmed
Threshold – the entrance to a house
Toddler – a young child, just a little older than a baby
Toppled – fell over
Tripod – a three-legged stand that a camera sits on
Tyke – a little child
Utterly – absolutely, completely
Vantage point – a position for viewing something
Wretched – upset
Yelped – to make a sharp cry